COOPER

meet cooper

montse ganges

emilio urberuaga

Published in 2009 by Windmill Books, LLC
303 Park Avenue South, Suite # 1280, New York, NY 10010-3657

Copyright © Combel Editorial, S.A.
Copyright © Montse Ganges (text)
Copyright © Emilio Urberuaga (illustrations)
Credits: Written by Montse Ganges
         Illustrated by Emilio Urberuaga

                    Publisher Cataloging Data
Ganges, Montse
       Meet Cooper / M. Ganges and E. Urberuaga.
              p. cm. – (Cooper)
       Summary: Simple text and illustrations introduce Cooper the dog and his likes
and dislikes.
       ISBN 978-1-60754-233-9 – ISBN 978-1-60754-234-6 (pbk.)
ISBN 978-1-60754-235-3 (6-pack)
       1. Dogs—Juvenile fiction   [1. Dogs—Fiction]   I. Urberuaga, Emilio   II. Title   III. Series
       [E]—dc22

Printed in the United States of America

For more great fiction and nonfiction, go to www.windmillbooks.com.

alphabet
s o u p

an imprint of

WINDMILL
BOOKS
New York

Cooper likes sunny places.
They make him sleepy.
He doesn't like it if you
blow air on his nose.
That makes him sneeze.

Cooper likes people
to walk with him.
He doesn't like to be left
alone in a field of tall grass.

Cooper likes to
dig in the dirt.
He doesn't like smooth,
slippery floors.

6

Cooper likes the toy
that goes SQUEAK!
when you squeeze it.
He doesn't like fireworks.
They frighten him.
A lot.

Cooper doesn't like it to
start raining when he's
about to go for a walk.
But he enjoys drying himself
by racing up and down the
sidewalk at full speed.

Cooper likes to hypnotize people.
He stares at people when
they are eating and thinks:
"Give me the steak!"
He stands in front of people
when they are reading and thinks:
"Take me for a walk!"
And sometimes it works.

He loves balls that
bounce like crazy.
But he doesn't like
balls that are too big.

He likes to be invited
onto the sofa.
"Come on, Cooper!"
He doesn't like it when
he has to get down.
"Down, boy!"

He likes to see the world.
But he doesn't like going in the car
(mainly because they never let him drive).

18

He doesn't like baths or soap.
He likes puddles and mud.

He doesn't like it
when the TV barks.
He likes to play with Aunt
Lily's Great Dane puppy.

He likes to welcome people.
He doesn't like it when people say
goodbye. So make him happy
and come back again soon!